JUV
FIC

Peck, Robert Newton.

Higbee's Halloween.

$13.95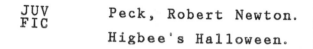

DATE			

Higbee's Halloween

Books by
Robert Newton Peck

A Day No Pigs Would Die
Path of Hunters
Millie's Boy
Soup
Fawn
Wild Cat
Bee Tree
Soup and Me
Hamilton
Hang for Treason
Rabbits and Redcoats
King of Kazoo
Trig
Last Sunday
The King's Iron
Patooie
Soup for President
Eagle Fur
Trig Sees Red
Basket Case
Hub
Mr. Little
Clunie
Soup's Drum
Secrets of Successful Fiction

Trig Goes Ape
Soup on Wheels
Justice Lion
Kirk's Law
Trig or Treat
Banjo
Soup in the Saddle
Fiction is Folks
The Seminole Seed
Soup's Goat
Dukes
Spanish Hoof
Jo Silver
Soup on Ice
Soup on Fire
My Vermont
Hallapoosa
The Horse Hunters
Soup's Uncle
My Vermont II
Arly
Soup's Hoop
Little Soup's Hayride
Little Soup's Birthday
Higbee's Halloween

Higbee's Halloween

by Robert Newton Peck

Walker and Company
New York

First published in the United States of America in 1990
by Walker Publishing Company, Inc.

Published simultaneously in Canada by Thomas Allen & Son
Canada, Limited, Markham, Ontario

Library of Congress Cataloging-in-Publication Data
Peck, Robert Newton. R0088830560
Higbee's Halloween / by Robert Newton Peck.
Summary: Life in quiet Clod's Corners changes drastically for
Higbee and his best friend Quincy when the very nasty Striker kids
move in and Higbee decides to make them the target of a grand
Halloween prank.
ISBN 0-8027-6968-3.—ISBN 0-8027-6969-1 (reinf.)
[1. Halloween—Fiction. 2. Behavior—Fiction.] I. Title.
PZ7.P339H1   1990
[Fic]—dc20   90-12712

Printed in the United States of America

2   4   6   8   10   9   7   5   3

C H A P T E R

1

"Ouick," said Higbee, "there it goes."

In pursuit, I nosedived into the brown October grass and tall weeds, all my talons extended, grasping at straws.

"Shoot," I said. "I missed it."

"Quincy," said Hig, "it's over here."

He dived too. Our prey wasn't easily caught. Critters as slippery as this seldom are. But between Higbee's hands and mine, we cornered it. Our captive lay helpless and, more importantly, unharmed.

"I got it," I said, grabbing its tail. This was easy, because it had a very very very long tail.

"Quincy," said Hig, "you're a regular Mr. Frank Buck, that famous big-game hunter we saw in the movies last summer, remember? He cap-

tured all those African lions . . . alive. Got an empty pocket?"

In several places I felt the bulging denim of my overalls. "No, not really. My pockets are full up with necessary stuff for school." You know, like marbles, a sardine can key, innertube rubber for slingshots, my arsenal of brook pebbles, Hig's jackknife and mine, a few bottlecaps, gum wrappers to smell when I don't have a penny, acorns, horse chestnuts, shortstop bubblegum cards, plus an old report card from last year.

Higbee sighed.

"Okay," he said, "put it in *my* pocket."

Carefully, tenderly, I eased our newfound captive into the bib pocket of his overalls, directly south of his chin. Hig snapped the flap securely closed.

"There," he said. "Snug as a bug."

"Now," I said, "we've got to get going to school."

We hustled on, along a dirt road toward a one-room brick schoolhouse, to Miss Wiggleton (the only teacher) and her stratospheric standards of education, hygiene, and deportment.

Our morning seemed to drag by with all the speed of an aging and arthritic snail. Some delivery guy stopped by to unload a small package and several kids surged forward to help Miss Wiggleton unwrap the parcel. It was only textbooks, in which Hig and I had little interest.

"Now's our chance," said Hig. "Let's do it, Quince."

We did it. It only took about ten seconds to pull off our caper. As I flipped open Bruto Bigfister's lunchbox, Higbee slipped our squirming surprise inside. Quickly we closed the lid.

"There," he said, "the joke's on Bruto."

Yet our day hardly turned out as rapturously as Hig and I had planned. Because one second after school was over, we both were in trouble, and running for our lives. Bruto was after us! Emily Turner had told him that she'd seen Higbee Higginbottom and Quincy Cobb (me) sneak a surprise into the lunchbox, between his toad sandwich and his brass knuckles.

"Don't look back," Hig panted.

But I looked back. Bruto was gaining!

If he caught us, there'd be a lot of blood spilled. My blood and Hig's blood. Bruto Bigfister was the toughest and meanest kid in town. He was built thicker than a rodeo bull (both had a cloven hoof) and with breath toxic enough to corrode a sewer grate.

Sometimes we called him . . . The Brute.

Or other things.

Banking left, we ducked under the pine board fence behind Thurber's Tool Works and into a back alley. Higbee wheezed to a stop, closed an eye, and squinted through a knothole.

"Is he coming?"

3

Hig winced. "Like a cavalry charge up San Juan Hill."

He backed away from the knothole and I looked. Bruto was coming for certain, his chunky legs churning like truck pistons, his face frozen into a frown of ferocity.

His fists doubled.

Then tripled.

The last time Higbee and I had been caught by Bruto Bigfister, he sat on us, removed Hig's trousers and mine, and tossed them on the roof of a bus that was pulling out of town, headed for Buffalo.

"Quincy," said Hig, "let's get out of here."

We ran.

Luckily for us, it wasn't hot. It was October's crimson end, Indian Summer weather, mild until sundown, after which the night often flirted with frost. Leaves on our maples had ripened to red, pumpkin orange, yellow, and a russet brown. And if Bruto caught us, I knew, we too would change color.

To black and blue.

Until today, nobody had ever dared to put a snake into Bruto's lunchbox. He was feared for good reason. The Brute could chew up a railroad spike and then spit out thumbtacks. In appearance, he looked a lot like the infamous gangster Al Capone, yet he lacked Al's compassion.

Hig, on the other hand, was my very best pal.

He was also my neighbor, a year older than I

4

was, and he possessed an uncanny knack for plunging the pair of us into a pit of problems. Hig's real name was Higbee H. Higginbottom. Yet near to everybody in our town of Clod's Corner called him Hig . . . plus a few alternate and less endearing terms.

Together, we tore through the back alley, ducking behind the backsides of a row of small stores, rounding another corner. Pulling to an out-of-breath whoa behind Holman's Candy Store, we paused to inhale some necessary oxygen, then pushed onward. We didn't dawdle until we'd made it over another fence and into the shadows of Ridgeway's Dry Goods.

Entering the store was out of the question. A week ago, old Flint Ridgeway had collared the two of us and removed us from his establishment, merely because he'd caught Hig in the ladies' department, trying on a corset. Some people just don't have much of a flair for comedy.

Right then, as Hig and I had paused for breath, something rather weird happened.

The back door of the dry goods place opened, and a naked person flew out. I mean *flew*. The naked somebody landed on a pile of junk. Then the door closed. I stared, unable to believe what I saw, because the naked person wasn't either a man or a woman. It was sort of a pink plaster thing. Studying the face, I knew I'd seen it before, yet couldn't quite remember exactly where.

5

"Hey look, Quince. It's a dummy."

"A what?"

"A mannequin. A fake person. Mr. Ridgeway uses them out front, in the store window, to wear clothes for sale. He must be throwing this one away. That's why there's no clothes on it. And no wig."

"Great, but Bruto'll be here in about ten more seconds. And when he gets here, there won't be anything on *us*. Except lumps."

Hig snapped his fingers. "Quince," he said, "I got it."

"*We're* going to *get it* if he catches us."

"Come on," Hig told me, "give me a hand." Moving quickly to the store mannequin, Hig snapped off an arm, a leg, and the bald head. "Quincy, help yourself."

I helped myself . . . to the other leg and other arm.

"What'll we do with these?"

"Hurry," said Hig. "We'll crawl under all this trash, and leave the arms, legs, and head sticking out."

Into Mr. Ridgeway's rubbish pile we leaped, leaving the mannequin's parts (four limbs and a head) exposed.

"Pray," whispered Hig. "Pray as if religion just got itself invented." I prayed. "And whatever you do, Quincy . . . don't make a doggone sound. Pretend you're a dead mouse."

"Why a mouse?"

6

"So," said Hig, "the *rat* doesn't hear us."

Sure enough, a rat named Bruto Bigfister came scrambling up and over the fence. It was a rare sight. The Brute seldom bothered to climb a fence. He usually punched his way through it.

"Okay," I heard Bruto's familiar snarl, "I know it'd be youse two stinkers who put that snake into my lunchbox. And I'm gonna ring your bells until you maybe think it's Sunday morning."

I shuddered.

It was only a *little* garter snake. Yet, to Bruto Bigfister, it might as well have been a thirty-foot python. To him, little things meant so much.

"Aha," I heard Bruto exclaim. "Just what I like twisting . . . a kid's arm."

Sure enough, he had spotted an arm. Grabbing, he twisted. Hard. Luckily, it wasn't my arm, or Hig's. It belonged to the store mannequin. However, I winced, hoping a mannequin couldn't feel pain. With one uppercut, Bruto could draw blood from a fire hydrant.

"Holy kimono," I heard him say.

Peeking out from under the trash, I saw Bruto holding a plaster arm and scratching his confused infested head. Just to make certain, Bruto took a bite out of the arm. Then he tossed it away and snorted out a swear word. A real zinger! But to me, almost everything Bruto said sounded like cussing, even if all he demanded was . . . "Hey, I'm hungry. Gimme your football."

I remained silent.

So did Higbee.

Our patience was rewarded. The Brute left as noisily as he had arrived and good fortune once again smiled on Higbee and me.

We had endured another day.

"Quincy," said Hig, as he crawled out of the trash, stood up, then looked at the mannequin parts, "these arms, legs, and head might come in handy."

"For what?"

"Maybe," said Hig, "we could find some sort of a use for them. So let's take 'em along."

We took them.

As Higbee and I both lived on farms, we had to be home by chore time. Five o'clock. So we climbed Homer's Hill in a hurry. In Mr. Haddock's cornfield he had dried corn shocks bound together, all standing freely here and there, like a crowd of tall ragged people wearing feathery hats. On the ground, pumpkins were everywhere, waiting to be harvested and then cut up for pies.

Hig pointed.

"Quincy, old bean, see that gully over there? That might be a perfect place to hide our mannequin parts."

Climbing over the gray rails of the cornfield fence, we approached the gully. And right then, my eyes almost popped out. So did Hig's. I couldn't be-

lieve what I saw. It was growing in the gully. Never had I seen one so large.

A giant pumpkin!

"That's got to be," Higbee said, "the most ponderous vegetable ever grown in the entire state."

We hid our mannequin parts under some fallen October leaves. We also added more to completely hide the pumpkin.

"Quincy," said Hig, "it would be a shame for Mr. Haddock to harvest this monster. Maybe we ought to do a good deed, and *rescue it*. Because this prince of pumpkins deserves to be more than just a big jack-o-lantern. It ought to be something more. You know."

I thought I knew.

It was *pie*.

CHAPTER 2

"Pie," said Miss Wiggleton.

It was the next day, in school.

Our extra-large-size teacher was grinding the gears of arithmetic, a boring subject about which I knew little. Just enough to get by. Higbee had taught me to count . . . from two (a deuce) all the way up to jack, queen, king, and ace. Up front, Miss Wiggleton mentioned a couple of people named Circumference and Diameter.

To me, all those Greeks were strangers.

Miss Wiggleton had drawn a big circle on the blackboard. The *pie* part, I concluded, was obviously about a pumpkin pie, because Halloween was only a few days off.

My attention left the blackboard at which Miss

Wiggleton was now standing, as my eyes were somehow wandering in the direction of the light of my life.

Her name? Mona May Winker.

Unknowingly, I was appraising her circumference, her diameter; not to mention her eyes. They were so blue that they made a cloudless sky appear to be, by comparison, almost green. All this, plus hair of golden flax.

I sighed, whispering her name as though it was an evening prayer, a vesper, an exhaled hymn.

"Mona May Winker."

Having overheard my intimate devotions, Hig glanced at me with obvious disgust.

"And," said Miss Wiggleton, her clacking chalk merrily grinding into academic dust, "if we use twenty-two over seven, which is of course a simplification, we can apply *pie* in a numerical formula." She drew an outhouse, a very tiny one, on our blackboard. "That," she announced, "is the Greek symbol of pie."

Hig elbowed me in the ribs. "Quincy, that's useful."

"An outhouse? It sure is."

"I meant useful in case we might want to measure our prince of pumpkins."

Right then, at that very moment of time, I somehow knew that my pal, Higbee H. Higginbottom, was about to hatch Halloween havoc. Trouble now seemed to occupy the ozone we were breath-

ing, as though it were a foul fragrance to further the folly of fools.

"So," said Miss Wiggleton, returning her stub of white blackboard chalk into its customary rut, "that's enough arithmetic for today."

I could not have agreed more.

Arithmetic, I had long ago concluded, was some mysterious method of medieval mayhem, or torture, devised by Sir John Napier (or some other Greek) to torment a farm kid like me. Besides, old Mr. Napier wasn't even famous enough to be on a bubblegum card . . . like Tyrus Raymond Cobb.

Outside, a car horn honked.

At once I recognized the familiar sound. A happy one. You can't mistake the *ooo-ga* of a Chandler car horn.

Sure enough, in less than a minute, in pranced a very small lady. It was Miss Booky, our librarian, who happened to be one of Miss Wiggleton's best friends.

"Salute me," Miss Booky exclaimed.

Miss Wiggleton saluted, with a smile on her face, coupled with a look of curiosity.

"I did it," Miss Booky announced to us all.

"Well," our teacher asked, "what did you do?"

Miss Booky sighed, sat on the edge of Miss Wiggleton's desk, and shot all of us a broad smile. "I just came from a meeting of the town committee. I'm the only woman on it."

"And?" Miss Wiggleton inquired.

"They were all dead set against it."

Miss Wiggleton saddened. "As they always are."

"Ah," said Miss Booky, jumping to her feet, "but I talked them into it."

Miss Wiggleton smiled. "I'm sure you did. What, pray tell, did you talk them into?"

Our librarian almost danced. "A Halloween party!"

Hig looked at me. And I looked at him. Things, I decided, were sort of *looking up.*

Back and forth, in front of us all, Miss Booky paced, crackling with enthusiasm and exuberance.

"It'll be Halloween night," she said. "Instead of all these young rascals going out and raising . . . well, you know . . . raising holy H . . . we'll have a Halloween party for the whole doggone town. Young and old. For kids of all ages."

"Where?" Miss Wiggleton asked her.

"On our village square."

A Halloween party, I was now thinking, was bound to be one heck of a lot of fun.

"And," said Miss Booky, "we'll make sure the party goes over with a *big bang.* To my recollection, nobody's bothered to shoot off our historic cannon in years. Not even last Fourth of July. So we're going to stoke up Big Mouth for Halloween."

Our teacher agreed.

Miss Booky, I could see, now had a bit in her teeth, and was galloping into high gear, hands ges-

turing, and eyes twinkling. You had to give Miss Booky credit. When it came to planning town fun, our free librarian was always enthusiastic.

"Yessiree," she said, smacking an open hand with her opposite fist, "Clod's Corner's old bronze howitzer just might get a workout. That is, if Lem Crocker can manage to remember where he stored that barrel of black powder."

Miss Booky pranced over to our only window, looked out, and then returned. "So," she said, "if the fair weather holds, we'll enjoy one boomer of a party. But that's not all of my good news."

Higbee nudged me. "There's more?"

I nodded. "Reckon so."

"It might be possible," Miss Booky almost whispered to our schoolroom of twenty-eight pupils, "that a rather *famous person* just might make it here to Clod's Corner, to be the guest-of-honor at our Halloween party."

"Who?" we all asked, even Miss Wiggleton.

"Well, I can't quite say for certain," our librarian replied, "but it could well be a very special somebody from Siberia whose name, here, and possibly in a few more distant locations, is darn close to being . . . a household word."

Miss Wiggleton took a step closer to her best friend, as though suddenly quite interested. "Are you going to tell us?"

Miss Booky shook her head. "Of course. But I honestly can't today. It's still sort of up in the air."

"Give us a hint," said Higbee . . . "Please."

Miss Booky paused.

"Okay. Our special visitor for the Halloween party won't quite be Mr. John Philip Sousa himself. *But*," she held up an encouraging finger to point at the ceiling, "this is a clue, an important one, to assist your guessing as to who's coming to town."

"Quincy," said Hig, "you know John Philip Sousa."

I looked at him blankly.

"I do?"

Hig nodded.

"Yeah. Everybody does. He's some sort of a king. It might be that he's a February king, or a March king. Maybe it was even as late as April. But my guess is March."

"I've got to run," said Miss Booky. "I'm due at the Free Library ten minutes ago, but I just had to pop around and tell the youngsters all the exciting news."

She headed for the door.

Miss Wiggleton went along with her.

Miss Booky stopped. "Just to be on the certain side," she said, "best I tell all three of them. So *one* of them'll remember to do it."

"To do what?" asked our teacher.

"Well, to make sure the cannon's loaded with gunpowder by Halloween night. So I'll instruct Lem Crocker, Melvin Murphy, and Osgood Keeler. And maybe even a few others."

After our librarian had cranked up her Chandler, choked it again, started it, and then finally took her leave, Miss Wiggleton turned to all of us. "John Philip Sousa," she said. "Who is he?"

All of us remained quiet.

Hig raised a hand.

"Higbee . . ."

"Miss Wiggleton, he's some sort of a famous gentleman who's a king. Isn't he?"

To my surprise, Miss Wiggleton smiled and nodded.

"Indeed so. Mr. John Philip Sousa, until the time of his death which was, as I recall, only a few short years ago, was known as the March King. He composed many stirring marches for all of America's marching bands to play."

"He can't come to Clod's Corner if he's dead, can he?" I asked.

"No, he can't, Quincy. But perhaps, in some fashion, he might come in spirit. After all," Miss Wiggleton's voice lowered to a ghost-story level, "spirits, some people claim, do often return on one special October festival." Her voice softened. "Some very weird monsters may come to town . . . for . . ."

"Halloween," yelled Higbee.

16

CHAPTER 3

Miss Wiggleton had been right.

She usually was. In fact, I couldn't possibly re-call a time when our teacher had guessed wrong about anything at all. Including whether or not I'd washed. I believed in Miss Wiggleton as much as (believe it or not) she believed in *me*.

Ghosts or ghouls or goblins would have been less frightening than guppies, compared to what came to Clod's Corner prior to Halloween.

Not even *Miss Wiggleton herself* could have pre-dicted that seven of the most meanest monsters would leave Siberia (a nearby town) and suddenly migrate to Clod's Corner, move in, and attend our little one-room school. They were so weird that, by comparison, Bruto Bigfister began to look normal.

And even *he* hated them enough to forget about us for a while, which we didn't exactly mind.

Actually, they were all Bruto's cousins, yet the name of this new family wasn't Bigfister.

It was Striker.

The family, perhaps more aptly called a *rat pack*, was composed of a father, Bubonico Striker, a mother named Convulsia, and seven of the rottenest and smelliest and sneakiest kids this side of Singapore. Their names had an uncanny way of becoming memorable, sticking into you like splinters.

In alphabetical and chronological order . . . Canker, Fester, Hernia, Jaundice, Scurvy, Typhus, and Zitt.

Even though Zitt was the youngest, and smallest, he was easily the most ornery . . . because the older six had pelted and pounded him since he was born. Zitt, even though only half the size of Bruto, could destroy him in a fair fight. Not that Zitt, or any other Striker, even once considered fighting fair.

The Striker children all carried matches.

In one day, they torched The Dump, the sawdust pile by our local sawmill, Miss Wiggleton's wastebasket, and their very own house at 666 Elm Street.

Striker boys chewed tobacco. Striker girls didn't. Instead, they smoked cigars.

Whenever they spoke, their language was cussy enough to shock a motorcycle gang, or to cause a

lumberjack to blush. Canker Striker told several of the chubby kids that they'd eventually turn to lard; and when that happened, the skinny kids like Higbee and me would have to eat them. Raw. Or feed them to pigs.

At Glotzenheimer's Grocery, Fester shoplifted six oranges, a dozen apples, and tried to stuff a watermelon into his underwear. Hernia, inside Holman's Candy Store, ripped off a box of long black licorice whips, and flogged every kid she could capture.

The Strikers never stole any baseballs. Only the bats, which they used to whack each other.

From the drugstore, they lifted a pint bottle of rat poison; and from Noah's Pet Shop, they swiped a large white rat named Lucky . . . who wasn't.

The Strikers didn't drop a single ant down a kid's back, inside his shirt. No, not a single ant. It was always an *ant farm.*

People said Mr. and Mrs. Striker (Bubba and Con) were even weirder than their whelps.

Higbee and I figured that their cookbook, if they even owned one, must have read something like this:

1. Take a horse's hoof.
2. Remove shoe only if desired.
3. Add nuts, bolts, and turpentine.
4. Boil in medium-size garbage can.
5. Beat with a tire iron until tender.

During noontime at school, when the Strikers weren't spitting saliva, or beer, or tobacco, or dirty words at each other, they spat at everyone else.

At Harry's Hardware, it was Jaundice and Scurvy who managed to heist an entire box of firecrackers. They didn't *keep* any. Instead, they climbed up on the roofs of houses, late at night, and dropped them down hot chimneys.

No one in Clod's Corner slept with more than one eye closed. Residents began stringing barbed wire on their porches. And electrifying it.

The Strikers owned a dog and a cat, both of which were constantly teased, tortured, and tormented. Their dog, a lanky critter named Fang, didn't look at all like a dog. She resembled an alligator with its tail chopped off. Only Fang's jaws were bigger. Higbee and I took a liking to her, because Fang bit every Striker she could catch. Fang feared no living creature, man or beast, except one.

She feared Slasher.

Slash was the Strikers' tomcat that weighed in about a pound lighter than a Shetland pony. He earned his nickname by repeatedly practicing his favorite hobby. He'd climb a tall telephone pole, meowing pitifully until a fireman climbed a ladder to rescue him. Then Slasher would leap on the man's face.

As soon as the seven Strikers began frequenting our school Miss Wiggleton ceased being a teacher.

She became, out of necessity, a referee.

And a first-aid expert.

The gray metallic lid of our school medical kit was open far more often than closed. Because of the Strikers, half of our class wore bandages, many of us reeked with iodine, and three hobbled around on crutches. Bruises ranged from the size of a hockey puck all the way up to the grand prize, a black-and-blue souvenir, a welt that would dwarf a manhole cover.

During one of Miss Booky's brief visits, the Strikers nearly managed to drive our librarian crazy. Canker had painted his face green and it wouldn't wash off. Typhus performed his usual trick, holding his breath until he either threw up or passed out. Not to be outdone, Scurvy pinched herself all over to create nearly a hundred little red blotches. One of them, only one, she proudly showed to our librarian.

"Hey, lookit this'n here," Scurvy hollered at Miss Booky, hiking up her sleeve to expose a red-blotched wrist.

Squinting through her glasses, Miss Booky thoroughly inspected the solitary blemish at close range, exploring it with a gentle fingertip.

"Does it itch?" she asked.

"Nope."

"Is this the only one you have?"

"No."

"Where is your other one?"

"Here."

21

"So I see."

"And here . . . here . . . down here . . . and away up in here, and here, and on my . . ."

Miss Booky's eyes nearly popped.

Scurvy said, "I'm a pox. But don't worry. All the rest of us Strikers got 'em too."

Yesterday, Scurvy and Jaundice had set up their own commercial venture, out back behind the schoolhouse. They were piercing ears. *Whether you wanted them pierced or not.* And charging the victim a nickel a hole. Rarely was there only one hole per ear.

"Some of them holes is big enough to be worth," Typhus said, "a whole quarter."

Prior to the arrival of the Strikers, not a single girl in the school ever wore any lipstick. None. Hernia Striker was the first, along with both of her sisters, and one of her brothers. Lipstick was also used to create more red blotches in order to fan the rumor of some insidious epidemic.

Miss Wiggleton swallowed more Bayer that first week than I'd seen her take in five years.

"Scurvy, have you been piercing ears during recess?"

"Yeah. Business is pleasure."

"What are you doing it with? A needle?"

"This," Scurvy held up a corkscrew.

I thought Miss Wiggleton would faint. Yet, armed with generations of stalwart fortitude, she somehow held on. Wrestling the corkscrew away

22

from Scurvy, our teacher dropped it into a lower drawer of her desk.

Miss Wiggleton didn't bother to help herself to any more aspirin. Her bottle was empty. But the next day she brought in a new supply.

A bigger bottle.

CHAPTER 4

School ended.

Twenty-six kids exploded out the door; and Miss Wiggleton, after shaking our hands, sank slowly into her desk chair. She looked out of gas and ready to be put up on blocks.

Our teacher's face was wearing neither a smile nor a frown, but merely a blank expression, one which contained all the voltage of a dead battery.

Hig and I stayed a minute or so, to assist her. It wasn't that we *had* to stay after school. We both agreed we'd do it, to help out, on account that Miss Wiggleton had been doing such a bang-up good job handling all seven of those Strikers.

"This too shall pass," I thought I heard our teacher say.

The two of us, Higbee and I, made short work of the afternoon chores. Compared to farming, emptying a waste basket, washing a blackboard, and dusting a brace of erasers amounted to next to nothing at all.

It wasn't the first time we stayed.

Neither my pal nor I mentioned it out loud. Yet inside, I sort of had me a hunch that Higbee H. Higginbottom and Quincy Cobb treasured Miss Wiggleton as somebody really special. She wasn't any ordinary person. Instead, she was a *teacher.* Our teacher. The only teacher that I had, during my brief span of life, ever known.

She was on *our side.*

No, not in the sense of tossing a baseball bat and then choosing up sides outdoors behind the school. It ran deeper than that, beyond my ability to explain it to anybody. Not even to Hig. Never, not once in my entire life, had I ever hit a homer. Perhaps because I wasn't strong enough, or tall, or big enough. Yet, if I had hit one, Miss Wiggleton would have cheered, and clapped, and certainly informed me that she knew I could spit on a bat handle and smack one over the fence . . . *me,* Quincy Cobb.

At night, whenever I went to sleep, I could always close my eyes and know that, of all the twenty-eight kids in our school, Miss Wiggleton liked *me* the best.

No, that's wrong.

25

She loved me the most.

It wasn't as though she'd said so. But, deep inside me, my feelings hugged her as though she belonged to us, as we all belonged to her. Not in a hundred years would I ever dream of admitting my secret thoughts to Hig. Yet I didn't have to. Inside my pal, I sort of knew that he was feeling the same doggone way, holding Miss Wiggleton like a prize that you'd find on a cloud.

"Quince," he asked, "are you finished?"

Whacking two erasers together, and seeing all that chalkdust fly up and out, I nodded to my friend.

"Nearly," I told him.

"Okay," said Hig, "let's head uproad."

At her desk, Miss Wiggleton rewarded each of us with a benevolent glance. Not a genuine hip-slapper of a county fair blue-ribbon grin. Only a gentle soft smile. In her fashion, her expression told us that she was thankful we'd had the gumption to stay behind, to help out. Without coming right out and saying so. She didn't have to. We knew.

"Good-night, Miss Wiggleton," said Higbee.

I said likewise.

Funny, but she didn't actually answer. All she did was stand up, walk to us really slow, and touch our faces. And then she said something that I didn't quite savvy. Only two words, as her hands lingered on our cheeks.

"My reward," she said softly.

On the way home, Hig and I decided to cut through downtown, in order to help ourselves to a quick look-see at Big Mouth, the impressive hunk of bronze that commanded our village square in Clod's Corner.

There it stood.

Our cannon.

"Wow," said Hig. "Every time I see this giant gun I sort of start feeling proud. How about you, Quincy?"

"Me too."

Without as much as a by-your-leave, I kicked up my right leg in order to vault myself up atop the bronze barrel. I was straddling it like a cowboy sits his horse. Beneath me, the big barrel felt cold, and harder than history.

More than a century ago, Mr. Titus Yuckerson Clod had donated this cannon to us all, to our town of Clod's Corner.

It all had something to do with the American Revolution, or so Miss Wiggleton had told us. Legend held that Titus, with a smoking pistol gripped in each paw, avoided the British Redcoats at the Battle of Clod's Retreat, and saved his entire brigade.

Regardless, here now stood Big Mouth.

Our giant cannon.

It was the village's single metallic remnant of flag-waving self-respect, our token of patriotism, proof that the blood that once gushed through ar-

teries now harder than the bronze upon which I sat, was, in essence, the noble wail of freedom, of liberty, of our community's cry of common cause.

Big Mouth, however, was a fake.

No real cannon, all of our village historians claimed, had ever been cast so large. Proof of its fakery was this. The hole. Big Mouth really did have a big mouth.

Humongous.

Higbee was up front, right now, peering into its darkness. Getting down from atop the barrel, I joined him, also to squint into the business end and into the endless black tunnel of nothing. Except mystery.

"Pie," said Hig.

He sometimes made odd remarks which zoomed in from left field, and meant litte, or nothing. This *pie* was probably one more of them.

"Quincy," he said, "did you hear what Miss Wiggleton happened to say today, in school, or were you too busily occupied in your devoted admiration of Mona May Winker?"

"Of course I heard it."

"Good," said Hig, "because what our teacher told us was concerning this very cannon, Big Mouth, our noble fieldpiece of yesteryear."

I looked at him blankly.

Higbee was again looking at the cannon's barrel, yelling "hello" into it, as though he suspected somebody was hiding inside. Then he turned to me,

and grinned. "Remember last March," he asked, "when Mrs. Murphy couldn't find her husband for three days, following Saint Patrick's Day?"

"I recall. Even our volunteer firemen were searching for Mr. Murphy, looking everywhere."

It was true.

Half the town had been peeking into crates, boxes, stairwells, barns, and chicken-coops, yelling, "Melvin Murphy . . . where . . . are . . . you?"

Hig patted the bronze cannon.

"And right inside here," he said, "they finally located Mr. Murphy, sleeping soundly, his big body occupying the barrel of our heritage."

I peeked in its mouth.

"In here?"

"Right. Lots of room in there. This gun is really big around. No wonder they never cast a lead cannonball for this old baby. It would have taken all the soldiers in the army to lift it up and load it."

"Well," I said, climbing up on the cannon barrel once again, a leg dangling down on each flank, "Miss Booky said that our village Halloween party ought to go over with a Big Mouth *bang*."

"I can't wait," Hig said. "When this cannon goes off, it'll bound to be some blast."

He suddenly began to search his pockets, then looked up at me.

"Quincy, old sport, seeing as you tote around so much junk, you wouldn't happen to have a tape measure, would you?"

29

I searched.

"No."

"Well, how about some string?"

That I had.

Passing it down to Higbee, I watched him stretch my length of dirty old string across Big Mouth's big mouth.

"How can you measure with a string?" I asked him.

"Easy. I'll tie a knot, and when you get the string home, lay it tight along a yardstick. Then, when I see you tomorrow, you can tell me how many inches across Big Mouth measures."

He tossed me my string.

That night, after my chores were done, supper eaten, and homework tackled, I fished the string from my pocket. Then I measured it, from end to knot, and mentally noted the result.

It was exactly twenty-one inches.

Before drifting off into sleep that night, I couldn't quite think about Mona May Winker. Instead, I was thinking about Higbee, and his surprising interest in the length of a piece of dirty old string.

Also I was thinking of another curiosity.

Pie.

CHAPTER 5

Halloween was almost here.

Only a few more days until October's festive finale, and the big party that Miss Booky had been planning. And touting.

"Now don't forget," Miss Booky informed everyone in Clod's Corner that she met on Main Street, "be sure to come in costume."

"Costume?" they'd ask.

"Sure. But it doesn't have to be anything fancy," she injected. "Just chase the kids up into the attic, open up some old trunk, and turn 'em loose. They'll wiggle into something spooky. On Halloween, I want everybody to be scared stiff."

Little did little Miss Booky know.

We kids were already near to scared out of our

skulls. Of ghosts? Of goblins? Of witches riding broomsticks at night across a full moon? Of black cats? No, none of the above. Or, if you're really into buried bodies, none of the below.

We had the Striker gang.

Even though the window of Newt's Novelty Shop featured a bloodcurdling congregation of hideous faces, all for sale, the Strikers wouldn't need any ugly masks. Their own faces were enough.

To make matters worse, smack dab in the center of Clod's Corner, the Strikers built their version of a fort.

A large shack.

They seemed to have constructed their building almost overnight, using old boards, busted crates, rope, garbage cans and trash bins, truck tires, gasoline drums, plus dug-up sections of a sewer pipe. The fort wasn't much to look at. Hardly anyone would include its photograph within a travel folder as one of our picturesque sights. Yet I couldn't help looking at it. Neither could Hig. We just stood and stared, hoping it would either tumble down or burn up.

It wasn't a castle for knights and fair ladies.

Not on your life.

The Strikers never called it so. Instead, their crudely constructed castle was known as . . . The Torture Chamber.

Zitt Striker had named their shabby shack.

It lived up to its name.

And his.

Inside, six Strikers were constantly ganging up on the unfortunate seventh, regardless of who it was. Also, any kid who wasn't a Striker, and happened to be stupidly strolling by, was nabbed, grabbed, jabbed, and then hauled inside for an hour of horror. Some concerned adults suggested to Mayor Doolittle that The Torture Chamber be torn down. Mr. and Mrs. Striker vehemently objected, claiming their kids had no place to play, and it also kept them out on the streets, and away from home.

Their neighbors reluctantly chimed in.

So the fort, or castle, or whatever sort of shack it was, was permitted to stay. It stood. A grim warning to any small potential victim that it was a pitfall to avoid. Kids, with any brains at all, ran past it at full throttle, as Higbee and I certainly did. Shuddering as we ran.

You didn't have to be captured to be hurt.

The Strikers had assembled an arsenal of objects to throw . . . rotten eggs, broken bottles, a carton of sour milk, various forms and weights of scrap iron, as well as the proverbial sticks and stones, to break people's bones.

Higbee had been hit by a flying frying pan.

I by a billiard ball.

Alfy Alfredo had been mashed by a potato masher. And even big Bruto had gotten bombed by a small bag of fertilizer. Only a devil would throw a sack of fertilizer marked 6-6-6.

The Strikers needed no party.

To them, every day was Halloween. Every trick a treat.

Mayor Doolittle had apparently decided to do little. Or nothing. Bubonico Striker, and his wife Convulsia, had no doubt frightened him into taking no action. The mayor mumbled something about "due process," because our mayor was a lawyer, a full partner in a local law firm.

Gyppum, Lotz & Cheatem.

Others in Clod's Corner thought that the Striker fort was merely a House of Horrors erected especially for Halloween, to amuse the local children. In fact, many adults laughingly gathered outside to listen to the shrieks and screams.

"Sounds almost real," a passerby commented.

Several concerned parents, along with their bruised, limping, and newly colored children, complained to the person who really ran the town, Miss Booky. Yet our librarian was so busily engineering the Halloween party that she couldn't afford to devote the time for demolition of demonic devices.

So it stood.

The Striker structure.

Hig and I spied on it, and its seven sinister occupants, from a safe distance, lying flat on the roof of Darby's Grain & Feed. We saw that the Strikers were rarely as nasty to outsiders as they were to each other.

"We can't see very much from here," Hig said,

"so maybe we ought to work ourselves forward for a closer look-see."

"No," I said. "Please, no closer."

Hig winked. "Quincy, what would Mona May Winker say if she suspected that you're afraid of the Strikers?"

"Well, she'd probably think that I had a sense of self-preservation. Dead heroes," I told Hig, "never get to marry pretty girls."

"Yuk," said Hig, suddenly standing up, "enough about marriage. You know I have a weak stomach. Let's move in a roof closer."

I sighed. "Well, all right. Just this once."

Climbing down, we changed our spying location to the roof of our local fire station, home of our bravest in blue, the Clod's Corner Hook & Ladder Heroes, volunteer firefighters all. From where we were hiding on their roof, Higbee and I could squint through a crack in the skylight at what transpired below. It was nothing more than the usual poker game. No money, however, graced the card table.

Firemen play for matches.

Somewhere, underneath me, I heard a door slam. "Hey," a voice hollered. "It's come."

At the poker table, all of the firemen dropped their cards, hurrying away.

"What is it?" I whispered.

"Can't quite make it out," Hig said. "But the

35

gent who just arrived is José. He's carrying some sort of a package in a red wrapper."

"Look," I said. "They're undoing it."

Whatever it was, all of the firefighters seemed more than interested, as Captain José Hosea fumbled with the string. "I can't believe it," he kept saying. "It's been weeks and weeks, but now she's arrived at last." He yanked at the cord. "Golly, this doggone knot must've got tied by an Eagle Scout."

"Here," another fellow offered, flipping open his pocketknife, "try cutting it."

"Thanks."

Bit by bit, their mysterious package got opened. Heads, all huddling around the poker table, were bending down to inspect whatever it was our fire department had sent for.

"Ah," somebody said.

"Sure is a beauty," another added.

"And, to boot, she's bright red."

"Of course it's red," said Captain Hosea. "That's the only color it comes in. Equipment for a fire station doesn't ever come in pink or lavender."

"Wouldn't matter," said another voice, "what the doggone color is, as long as she blares out good'n loud."

Captain Hosea held it up for all to see.

"Now *that*," he told his volunteers, "is about the finest and best battery-powered bullhorn that money can buy. If there's a serious fire, we can employ our bullhorn to keep the crowd back."

36

"And," said somebody, "to direct traffic."

"Why, there's got to be a hundred useful uses for a good bullhorn."

"Especially," another man said, "if it's bright red."

Several voices mumbled their agreement.

"Red," said someone, "is a fireman's color. Did I ever tell you fellows about the crimson pajamas that Mildred bought me last year, for Christmas?"

"You told us. Every day."

"Nevertheless," said Captain José Hosea, using a more serious tone, "our new bullhorn is here. At last. And nobody could say that the town budget didn't get its money's worth."

The chatter below continued to exchange.

On and on.

"Quincy," said Hig, "you won't believe it."

"No, I probably won't."

He poked me in the ribs. "Listen up, Quincy. Perhaps, just perhaps, I may be hatching the master plan of my entire life."

Standing up quickly, I almost fell off the roof of the fire station, had Higbee Higginbottom not grabbed my belt and hauled me back.

"Please," I pleaded to Hig, as soon as I was able to swallow my fright and speak. "Please, no plans. Every time you plan a plan, the pair of us splash ourselves down into deep trouble. Remember the last time?"

Hig nodded, remembering. "How," he asked

me, "could I know it wouldn't glide off our barn roof?"

I winced. But then my curiosity overcame my caution. Inside, I somehow had to learn whatever it was that Higbee H. Higginbottom was now plotting.

"Hig, does it have to do with those Strikers?"

His face beamed slowly into a grin, as a full moon suddenly blooms from behind an evening cloud.

"Bingo," he said quietly. "You win."

CHAPTER 6

"Nifty news," said Miss Booky.

Higbee and I just happened to meet her on Main Street. Her face was beaming with joy.

"What is it?" Higbee asked.

Miss Booky gestured with an enthusiastic fist punching nothing except open air. "He's coming! All the way here from Siberia, and that's over twenty miles."

"Who's coming?"

Leaning forward, as though Miss Booky didn't want anyone else to overhear her secret news, she whispered a famous name:

"Schwarzenegger."

Neither Hig nor I could even breathe. Were my

ears playing tricks on me? Could it really be true? Was *he* really coming here to Clod's Corner?

As if hearing my silent question, Miss Booky nodded. "Yep," she stated firmly, "he'll be here. For sure, he's coming to town. Mr. Splitlip Schwarzenegger."

"But," asked Hig, "will he bring it?"

"Oh, he'll bring it. I don't guess," Miss Booky assured us, "that Splitlip Schwarzenegger never travels even as far as the you-know-where without his sousaphone."

A few days ago, in school, Miss Wiggleton again had mentioned John Philip Sousa and the big bass horn he had invented. "Whenever we see a marching band go parading by," she had explained, "a sousaphone is easy to spot. Because it's the band's biggest instrument. Great circular tubes are winding around the sousaphonist's upper body. Over his head, there's a very large bell, from which come the notes, the deep booming sound."

In a parade one time, Hig and I had seen a sousaphone. Yet one of average dimension.

Everybody knew that Mr. Splitlip Schwarzenegger's instrument couldn't honestly be described as ordinary. He played the largest sousaphone ever manufactured. Splitlip was also, rumor held to be, a very large man.

A giant.

"Now don't tell," Miss Booky hushed as she

waved a warning finger. "Nobody in town is supposed to know. It's a surprise."

"We won't," he promised her.

We didn't have to share a word of it. Because, as she left us, Miss Booky went hurriedly down the street, telling everyone she met. And then cautioning people not to divulge her closely guarded secret.

"Wow," said Higbee, after she had disappeared from sight, "he's really coming to town."

Not much happened, entertainment-wise, in our sedate little village of Clod's Corner. Prior to the arrival of the Striker clan, life had been little more than a trio of school, chores, and bed. Except, of course, fending off the fists and fangs of The Brute. But the Strikers and their Torture Chamber, by contrast, managed to reposition Bruto somewhere between *Rebecca of Sunnybrook Farm* and *Heidi*.

Yet, as Hig was always claiming, it's a foul wind that breaks no good. So both of us enjoyed observing Bruto Bigfister in panic, for a change, and running for his life. He also feared The Torture Chamber.

Slowly the two of us walked uproad, toward home.

Higbee suddenly stopped.

"Bullhorn," he said.

I shot him a questioning glance.

"Quincy, my friend, we now must consider a

bullhorn, a length of old string, possibly a sousa-phone, one useless old bronze cannon for which there is no ammunition, plus an upcoming Hallow-een party." Higbee grinned. "Ah," he said, "my prank for Halloween is slowly beginning to jell in my brain."

Higbee's prank.

Those two words always seemed to create a chilling sensation along my spine. Winter in Octo-ber. If my pal was inventing a plan, in his jelly brain, *disaster* would follow closely behind. Yet in spite of sensible reasoning, my curiosity could no longer contain itself. How, I was then starting to wonder, could Higbee H. Higginbottom combine such an array of odd elements into a semblance of assembly?

Bullhorn, string, sousaphone, cannon, and our forthcoming Halloween costume party.

"One more thing," Higbee said.

"Well," I asked, "what is it? Tell me."

"Pie."

As we continued walking up the hill along the familiar gravel road, I amused myself by kicking a few pebbles. A pumpkin pie, I was then consider-ing, plus Mr. Splitlip Schwarzenegger was a cer-tain combination that one didn't encounter every day. To further confuse matters, Higbee again spoke.

"Quince, it just might work."

"What'll work?"

"A chain. That's the crux of my entire, yet possibly brilliant, idea. One can't handle it alone. Because there has to be a *chain*."

"Okay," I told him. "A chain it is."

To my mind, nothing whatsoever was making any common sense at all. Not in the least. Higbee's crazy schemes rarely did.

He looked at me. "You still have that length of string, don't you?"

I felt inside my pocket.

"Yup."

"Good. Fetch it here. Before we can form any further steps, I best discover if that string of yours is the right length."

Without another word, Higbee vaulted over the rail fence and into Mr. Hadlock's cornfield and pumpkin patch. My string trailed behind him like the tail of a kite.

"Be right back," Higbee said.

He returned smiling.

"We're in luck." He handed me the string. "Our prince of pumpkins may be closer to *pie* than you could ever begin to imagine. That's because of the figure sixty-six . . . in inches."

So many of Hig's enlightening explanations were no more than a muddying of curious water. Right now, nothing was clear. Not a word he'd said made any sense to me.

Sixty-six inches?

As we started homeward, Higbee said, "We'll have to start tonight."

"Start what?"

"Collecting all the necessary stuff."

"What do we need?"

"A pillow, some ratty towels or rags or even old clothes, and a very very very lengthy piece of . . ." Higbee looked my way. "Take a guess, Quincy."

"String."

"No."

"Chain."

"Nope. Wrong again."

"I give up."

"Wire," said Hig. "We'll require almost an entire coil of copper wire, yet long and sturdy."

"To do what?"

"We're going to construct something horrible."

"Well . . ."

"It's a *spook*."

Slowly I exhaled. A spook (whatever it was) didn't sound too dangerous. At least Hig's plan didn't involve our constructing a bomb. But the more I thought, the more my hands and neck began to sweat.

"What kind of a spook?" I asked Higbee.

"One," he said, "that will scare breakfast, dinner, and supper out of certain people, those intended to be our designated targets." Hig patted me on the back. "It'll take courage to perform *your* part of our capricious caper."

"Courage?"

"Indeed, and guts aplenty."

"I don't want to do it."

Hig stopped. "Of course you'll want to do it."

"Why?"

"Because," explained Higbee, "in a way, your target might be . . . *Mona May*." He sang her name with lace-edged notes.

"Mona May Winker?"

Hig shrugged. "Unless you know so many Mona Mays that it's difficult for you to sort 'em all straight."

Trudging along the gravel road, I was wondering what Higbee meant when he mentioned that Mona May would be my target. So I outright asked him.

He told me.

"In a way," said Higbee, "*she* will be your target, because you're bound to make a super impression on her . . . as soon as you crash land."

I asked no more questions. Mainly because I couldn't stand any of Hig's answers, none of which made me feel any safer.

"Poetry," said Higbee. He suddenly snapped his fingers. "That might possibly be the lucky link in our chain."

We stopped at my house.

"Hurry," said Hig. "I need a pencil and paper."

"What for?"

"A poem."

"For a girl?" I asked.

"No, for the Strikers."

It took me less than ten seconds flat to produce a hunk of paper and a short stub of a pencil. With his tongue in the corner of his mouth, Higbee began to compose, and write. Then he let me read what he had written. And, as he'd promised, his little verse was a poem, yet also a warning threat to those seven rotten little Strikers:

Unless you promise never to be mean, your Torture Chamber falls . . . on Halloween.

There was more than just the poem on the paper. Higbee H. Higginbottom had also printed the poet's name below.

It was signed . . .

The Spook

CHAPTER 7

I was dreaming.

And I could hear music.

In my dream, I wasn't Quincy Cobb. Instead, I was wearing a bright red-satin band uniform, marching in a parade along Main Street. And being John Philip Sousa.

My hands spun a shining silver baton, because I was the leader, the drum major. My uniform was fancier than all the others who marched behind me. My legs kicked higher and smarter as my baton was spinning a silvery circular blur. My whistle shrieked every cornering command with the blasting authority of a four-star general.

Everyone in Clod's Corner was cheering.

And then I spotted Mona May Winker.

She was waving to me, and smiling. But then she stopped waving and asked me, "Say, aren't you really Quincy Cobb?"

I shook my head.

"No," I told her. "I am Mr. John Philip Sousa, the March King, and all these musicians behind me are my band. My mother says that if they follow me home I can keep them."

Turning around, I happened to notice that my band was all male. All men. And each guy was a giant blowing a sousaphone. Yet one solitary horn seemed to be larger than all the others, and blowing louder notes. Big boomers that sounded as if coming not from a sousaphone but from a bronze cannon. Or a well.

"I know you," I said. "You are Splitlip Schwarzenegger."

"No," he said. "I'm not."

"Then who are you?"

"My name is . . . Zitt Striker." It was true. He started to look a lot like the youngest of the seven from Siberia. "In fact," said Zitt, "if'n you had brain, you'd take notice that we's all Strikers . . . everybody in the band."

I looked.

Zitt was right. They were Strikers all. I could tell because they were hitting each other, with sousaphones, and eating all the music.

I saw Miss Wiggleton standing between two foreign-looking gentlemen whom I recognized as

Circumference and Diameter. Behind them stood Miss Booky, who was busily applying a bandage to a wounded John Napier.

"Hi," I said.

"Pie," answered John mathematically.

"Quincy," someone else was saying. It was a familiar voice, one that almost forced me to drop my twirling silver baton. "Wake up, Quincy."

"No," I said, "I want to be John Philip Sousa."

"You're not. You are The Spook."

Slowly I started to recognize the voice. It was somebody I knew and knew too well. I heard it once again. A kid's voice.

"Quincy. Wake up."

Opening my eyes, I stared at my pillow. Where was I? Where? In my bed.

"Quince. It's me."

Moving slowly, I got up, then went to my bedroom window. Looking out, and then down, I saw somebody below me, standing on the ground and fully dressed. It was Higbee H. Higginbottom. He was holding a bag. I opened the window, wincing at the creaky-sneaky sound it made in the darkness, wondering if I'd managed to awaken the whole county.

"Hig?" My voice was softer than a prayer.

"Yes. I'm down here and all ready to go."

"It's the middle of the night," I whispered.

"I know. But I just couldn't sleep. Not a wink. I

kept lying in bed thinking about our plan to destroy The Torture Chamber."

Rubbing my eyes, I asked, "Do we have to demolish it *now*? Can't it wait until morning?"

Higbee shook his head. "Remember what Miss Wiggleton told us, about Mr. Thomas Alva Edison, and how he often invented all kinds of important stuff . . . *in the middle of the night*?"

"Hush, you'll wake up my folks. I remember."

"Okay, I'll hush, if you throw some clothes on and drag yourself down here. I can't wage a war against all those infernal Strikers by my lonesome. So pull your guts together and be a partner."

I sighed. "Okay."

Three minutes later I was sneaking down the stairs, avoiding the seventh one because, if stepped on, it screamed like a stomped cat.

Outside our house, Higbee waited, holding a burlap sack of something or other over his shoulder. "About time," he told me.

"What's up?"

"*You are* . . . finally. So let's be on our way," Higbee said, "because I overheard Pa telling Ma that the Frobishers are moving to Scanton."

"You mean they want to abandon their duck farm?"

"Come on. I'll explain it on the way."

We were cutting across our back pasture.

"Well," said Higbee, "it's Mrs. Frobisher who decided that she's going to give up her hobby."

"What was her hobby?"

"Pillows," said Hig. "She liked sewing up all kinds of fluffy pillows. And she always started from scratch, using duck feathers."

"For stuffing?"

"Right."

Higbee switched his burlap bag to his other shoulder, even though it didn't appear to be overly hefty.

I yawned. "You know, Hig, I really don't believe I'm actually losing a good night's sleep just to chase a lot of ducks."

In the dark, we climbed over our south fence, and then continued on our way.

"We're not going over there for ducks, Quincy."

"We're not?"

"No. We are going to make things."

I stopped. "At this hour?"

Hig smiled. "Of course. Far as I know, there's really no prescribed time of day, or night, for duck feather work."

Even before our arriving at the Frobisher place, I could smell them. Not the Frobishers. The ducks. Hundreds of them. Then, as we approached, I saw them. All white. And all asleep. One particular duck let out a nocturnal *quack* and then stilled. But the duck smell was so strong that I could practically hear it. It was an aroma strong enough to float a horseshoe.

To make matters worse, I realized, after a

downward glance, that I was standing in duck manure. Oh, how I was instantly wishing that I'd worn shoes.

I glanced at Higbee's sack.

"Hig, you better not be planning for us to steal a duck. If so, I don't want to play any part in duck thievery, or jail."

My friend raised a restraining hand.

"Don't worry," he said.

"Then," I asked, "what's inside your bag?"

Hig grinned. "Bags."

"Bags?"

"Right. That's exactly what I brought along in my bag . . . more bags."

"What for?"

"Pillows. There's feathers all over the place, as you can see, so all we have to do is harvest them. Then we stuff our empty bags until they become fat plumpy pillows, and go home."

Against my better instincts, I found myself at Frobisher's Duck Ranch, bending over in the dark to pick up duck feathers. And trying not to pick up, by mistake, a sleeping duck. Speaking of mistakes . . . it is a mistake to scoop up duck feathers at night, because you pick up a lot of other stuff.

Higbee did too.

Yet, all was going well. We had crammed feathers into three burlap bags and had started to fill a fourth.

That's when it happened.

Hig stepped on an unlucky duck.

It quacked, making me jump, which caused me to step on another sleeping duck. As far as I was concerned, in the past, some ducks are okay. Yet a sleeping duck resents being stepped on. And, as we discovered in about one second, if you trip over a duck, all of the other six hundred become really huffy about it.

Our world, Hig's and mine, suddenly turned into nothing but noise. Loud ear-splitting bedlam and irate poultry.

Higbee was saying, or yelling, something. Yet all I could hear was six hundred ducks, each one annoyed that one of their flock had been rudely awakened by a clumsy-footed feather filcher.

"Look," Hig yelled. He pointed.

At the Frobisher's house, an upstairs light clicked on and a window opened.

"Harry," I thought I heard Mrs. Frobisher holler, "that cussed fox is out yonder in our duck yard again. Fetch a gun."

A *gun*?

My feet wouldn't budge. All ten of my toes seemed to be frozen, or glued, in a good inch of muck enriched by duck.

"Run," Higbee said.

We ran.

WHAM . . . WHAM.

It must have been a double-barrel shotgun. Twelve gauge. Pellets, small ones, seemed to be fly-

ing everywhere, zinging, whizzing and whining over our heads as we fled through the night, toting three overstuffed pillows that bulged with duck feathers.

How the two of us escaped without being peppered with buckshot I will never know. Yet we scrambled over the fence, into the shelter of darkness, and trotted across our south pasture, to home. I was panting. So was Higbee. But we still held our three burlap bags stuffed with duck feathers. I could have, however, murdered good old Higbee Higginbottom right where he was standing.

"Well," said Hig, "we did it, Quincy. We really pulled it off, old buddy."

I frowned at him. "Yeah, and nearly got our you-know-whats shot off." Then I smiled. "But we somehow got away with it."

Higbee chuckled. "Easy as . . . pie."

CHAPTER 8

"Ah," said Higbee.

We were standing near Big Mouth, the large bronze cannon. Behind it, Hig was sighting over the top of its barrel to see where it was pointed.

I looked too.

Oddly enough, Big Mouth seemed to be aiming at a particular object far distant, one that had been sloppily built by the seven Strikers. The Torture Chamber.

"Too bad," I said to Hig, "this cannon is a fake and has no ammunition. If it was a real gun, we could shoot and The Torture Chamber would de-struct."

Higbee said nothing.

He seemed to be watching some activity near

the gazebo, an octagonal wooden bandstand about a hundred feet away on the village green. Miss Booky was there. She was busily supervising the hanging of black and orange Halloween streamers.

"This ought to look especially festive," she was saying, "because here on the gazebo platform is where Splitlip Schwarzenegger is going to play his sousaphone solo."

Higbee and I walked closer.

We watched them decorate for a minute or two.

"Quincy," said Hig, "we can't stand here and be idle, watching other folks prepare. We've got preparations of our own to tackle."

"We sure do," I said, unsure of what they'd be.

"First off," said Higbee, "we need a wire." He looked up at the long span between two nearby telephone poles. "And up there is wire aplenty."

Right then, along came an olive-green repair truck. A telephone lineman dismounted from the truck, strapped a pair of climbing spurs on his lower legs, then started to walk up the telephone pole.

Higbee and I watched him. Yet my pal appeared to be observing something else, farther away.

"Holy cow," Hig said with even more enthusiasm than usual, "would you take a gander at *that*."

As he pointed, I looked.

"I don't see anything," I said, "except a steep

hill that's covered with maple trees, and lots of colorful October leaves."

"Good," he said.

I looked at Higbee.

"Because," he went on to say, "if *you* don't see it, nobody else will. But it's there. Ready and waiting, perhaps forgotten yet longing to be rediscovered, and harboring a secret desire to be needed, to be . . .

"Stop," I nearly hollered.

He stopped talking.

"Thanks," I said. "I can't stand it when you launch into language like a pig into a trough."

"Why not?"

"Well," I said, "for starters, rarely do I know what you're so excited about, and it's all I can do just to shut you up, and to afford my eardrums a second of silence."

Higbee grinned. "Sorry, old chap. Sometimes the joy within me bubbles up, and I can't contain it all." He hauled in a deep breath. "If you're really interested, what I spotted, up there, just might turn out to be the one item that'll solve your major Halloween problem."

Facing him, I asked, "Problem?"

Hig nodded. "Now then, come Halloween night, *you're* going to be something very important." He gave me a friendly punch. "You sure are."

"I was planning on being a pirate."

Higbee shook his head. "Well, pirates are okay,

57

if you're one of the smaller kids. This year, however, your costuming will serve our proud little community of Clod's Corner in a far more noble capacity."

The telephone repair man had completed whatever he was tinkering with, atop the pole, and was slowly climbing down, his spurs puncturing the wood. Higbee walked over to the base of the pole. I followed. As the repairman entered his truck, Hig sort of went too. I didn't. But, while waiting outside I heard voices. Hig seemed to be asking a question. Leaving the truck, he pointed up the steep hill. The telephone man looked and then shook his head.

"No," he said, "it hasn't been used in years."

"Oh," said Higbee.

"In fact," the man continued, "one of these years, providing I can finally find a spare minute of time, I'm fixing to take it down."

Meanwhile, I scratched my head.

As I leaned against the left front fender of the repair vehicle, I wondered exactly what kind of deviltry Higbee H. Higginbottom was up to. Perhaps it was something connected to a telephone. Or a telephone pole. Squinting up the hill, I still saw nothing but an ordinary steep hill, with trees on it. Nothing more. Hig, however, had spotted something weird.

I felt a sudden chill.

A cold sweat. Plus the unmistakable smell of

trouble that seemed to be wafting into both of my nostrils . . . like the fumes of a run-over skunk.

Seeing the grin on Higbee's beaming face as he walked toward me, I could have bet I knew who that skunk actually was.

Out of the blue, he said, "Quincy, let's go look for some buckeyes. We'll need 'em."

Here, during September and October, all of the horse-chestnut trees were fully out in pod. The thorny green pods would turn brown, crack open, and horse chestnuts (or buckeyes) would drop. They were prettier than flowers, or jewelry, or even gold.

We each found a couple of dozen. Some we threw at each other. Buckeyes are excellent for ammunition.

With out pockets bulging, we sat under the tree, rubbing chestnuts along the little crack valley where our noses met our cheeks, to make the buckeyes shine. Human shoe polish, Hig so often called it.

"Girls don't ever do this," said Higbee.

"How do you know?"

"Well," he said, "have you ever noticed Mona May Winker doing it? Seeing as you watch her so doggone much, seems you ought to have about memorized every move she makes."

Shucking a stubborn buckeye, I popped out another prize nut, a real brown and silver beauty. "I don't watch her very much."

"No matter," Higbee told me. "Because on Halloween night, at the big village party, Mona May Winker will be watching *you*."

"Me?"

"Right as rain. Even though she won't realize that what she's staring at is Quincy Cobb . . . she definitely will be watching. In fact, so will just about everyone else."

Hig tossed a buckeye into the air, caught it, then juggled three of them for almost a full second.

Now, I figured, was the time. The moment to stand firm and resolute. "I'm going to be," I told him, "a pirate."

Higbee sighed.

"Suit yourself," he cleverly quipped. "But as Captain Kidd, you'll contribute little or nothing to our plan for revenge against all those Strikers."

Revenge!

Closing my eyes, I saw them all. Canker, Fester, Hernia, Jaundice, Scurvy, Typhus, and Zitt. It wasn't nice to hate people. Yet I had to confess that my emotions were coming a bit close to more than slightly disliking all of the Strikers and their heartless hankerings.

Shuddering, I remembered my twenty minutes as a captive in The Torture Chamber.

Something, I was concluding, had to be done.

Somebody must act!

"Higbee," I said at last, "if you and I are hon-

est-to-golly declaring a war on those rotten old Strikers, maybe I don't really have to be a pirate."

"Bully," he said, "I'll always count on *you.*"

"Well, what do I have to be?"

Turning to me, Higbee smiled.

"Quincy, old sport, the hour is nigh at hand for you to assume a new heroic identity, to become a character so frightening that you'll even curdle second-hand blood."

I flinched. "Nobody has blood like that."

"Somebody has second-hand blood. For sure."

"Who?" I asked.

"Dracula." As he spoke the name, Hig smiled at me. An evil smile, because he'd stuffed four pieces of candy corn between his teeth and gums, to look like vampire fangs. My bone marrow became frozen yogurt.

I said, "I don't like Dracula."

Higbee sighed. "A pity. He speaks so well of you."

"Okay, if whatever I do, and whoever I'll be, will help rid ourselves of all seven of the Striker brats, not to mention Bubonico and Convulsia . . . I'll do it." I clenched a determined fist.

Hig held out a hand.

I shook it.

"Quincy," he said, "I knew you'd be our hero."

"Hold it, Hig. Right now, I want to know who I'll have to become on Halloween."

Higbee grinned, then he answered.

"The Spook."

CHAPTER 9

"Pie," said Mona May Winker.

The two of us were helping Mr. Haddock load his pumpkins into the bin of a wagon that was hitched behind a team of bay horses.

Around us, the pumpkin field was freckled with pumpkins, pumpkins, pumpkins . . . orange and ripe, and ready for pies.

Whenever we came to a large pumpkin, Mona May and I would lift it up together. Sometimes, while performing this task, my hands would touch hers, underneath the pumpkin. As this daring intimacy transpired, I would look into Mona May's eyes, she into mine.

Few words were spoken.

Holding hands, beneath an October moon (or,

62

in this case, an October pumpkin) rarely needs a lot of language to smother so sugary a sensation.

Another thing that made me happy was the fact that Mona May's hands were, at the moment, as dirty as mine. This rarely happened. In the past, at school, Mona May Winker had pointedly commented that I was a very nice boy. But, she stated, if I used soap and water more often, I might even be nicer.

There was, I gradually began to suspect, a distinct difference between young males and young females. During first grade, I figured that *girls* were nothing more than *clean boys*.

Now, however, as my fingertips brushed hers, I was convinced that a special girl could become a whole lot like a special pumpkin.

Both made me feel orange all over.

"Quincy," she asked me in a soft willowy voice that could, at times, almost knot a sheepshank in my small intestine, "do you like pumpkin pie?"

I nodded, not trusting myself to speak.

We placed the pumpkin carefully in the wagon bin, atop the others, and returned to the vines for another.

"That's good," said Mona May, "because there's going to be a Pumpkin Pie Eating Contest at the Halloween party. Isn't that exciting?"

Again I nodded.

"And," she added, "wait until you see *the extra-*

special pie that's to be baked for the party. You'll never see a pie like it."

Bending low, Mona May picked up a pumpkin all by herself. It was one of considerable size. So I hefted up a pumpkin that was even bigger, to show her how strong I was. Turning, she started toward the wagon with her selection. I with mine. The first ten steps told me that perhaps I wasn't going to make it. I'd selected too heavy a pumpkin.

My arms were coming out of my shoulders.

Ahead of me, however, Mona May Winker marched forward bearing her burden as resolutely as if she'd been in boot camp training all summer with a crack platoon of Spartan infantry.

She even hummed.

I grunted.

Would it be possible, I was wondering, to drop the boulder of a pumpkin that I was toting, and quickly pick up a lighter one? Yes, I could pull it off. Because she was still walking ahead of me with her back turned. Now was my chance! I spotted a smaller pumpkin. Much smaller. So small that it could never pass for the one I was now struggling with, that felt like I carried a cow.

Darn it. She was actually singing.

No, there was nothing weak about Mona May Winker. Yet I couldn't let a *girl* win. She might tell all of the other girls, who would, in turn, tell all the guys.

Bravely I stumbled forward.

64

"Only another one hundred miles to go," my left arm seemed to be hollering to my right.

"I'll never make it," my right replied in a feeble and straining voice. "Go on without me."

Radishes.

Why? Oh, why didn't old Mr. Haddock grow radishes, instead of pumpkins? Closing my eyes, I could envision a green vegetable field, rife with radishes. And everywhere on Halloween night, tiny red radish jack-o-lanterns.

But radish pie?

"Quincy," I wheezed, "you can do it."

Below my chin, yet only an inch beneath, part of the stiff dried stem of the pumpkin I was transporting curled upward, almost like a welcoming handle. But I had no third hand. Both of my hands, now numb under a ton of orange vegetation, were cramped into prongs as rigid as those of a forklift truck.

Strange, but this particular pumpkin stem seemed a bit longer than usual.

Through eyes now watering and blurring in agony, I could barely make out Mona May Winker. And I absolutely did the impossible. I hated her. I actually hated her because of how she covered the last twenty feet of ground.

She was skipping.

Her feet seemed to dance through the field, flitting cheerfully along, carefree, lost in a dervish of which I couldn't share. Did I really hate her? Well,

no . . . not really. But I sure was beginning to hate my pumpkin.

It felt a lot more weighty than when I'd started. Was it possible? Did a pumpkin, even after it was picked from its vine, still continue to grow.

The vine, Vine, VINE.

It hit me!

That was it. In my haste to pick up a pumpkin, and walk to the wagon beside Mona May, I had overlooked one critical step. When picking my pumpkin I had forgotten to *pick* it. I hadn't bothered to separate it from the doggone pumpkin vine. No wonder it felt so stubborn.

I stopped.

Turning around, and looking back right then, I couldn't believe what I saw. How could I have done it to myself? Behind me trailed a pumpkin vine and several attached pumpkins, three or four of which were nearly as large as the one that was now breaking my backbone.

My knees jacked.

Or, seeing as it was the happy Halloween season, they both jack-o-lanterned.

I felt as though a pair of funny little faces were now being carved into both of my kneecaps. Inside my knees, two tiny candles were burning. Biting into the pumpkin stem, in order to snap it free of the vine, I said a bad word. "Schxptk." With my mouth full of gritty pumpkin stem, the word didn't sound as foul as intended.

"Come on, Quincy," sang Mona May, not a puff out of breath and sounding fresher than a May morning.

I moaned.

Step by step, I staggered toward her and the wagon, bearing my load. With unsteady steps, my feet somehow fought their meandering way forward, inch by inch. The last inch seemed to be unusually long (about a mile and a half) but I attacked its challenge.

"Here," said Mona May, unwittingly uttering what was the epitome of insult, "let me help you."

She helped me.

Suddenly the pumpkin became lighter, I grew stronger, my muscles flexed into knots harder than petrified grapes. At last the pumpkin was loaded.

"I'm glad you like pumpkin pie, Quincy. Because some of us girls, with help from our mothers, are going to bake all the pumpkin pies for the Halloween party."

I spat out flecks of pumpkin dirt. "Yuk," I said.

"Yuk?" One of her eyebrows arched in a practiced gesture of dismay. "Then no pie for *you*."

"Oh," I still spat, "I didn't mean yuk pie."

Her eyebrow slowly sank to normality. "I was hoping that the pie you'll eat might be the one *I* bake."

"Me too."

But at the moment, I really wasn't thinking about Mona May Winker. Almost *all* of Mr. Had-

dock's pumpkins were loaded into one wagon or another. All, that is, except for one.

The pumpkin in the gully.

Deep inside, I somehow knew that I wasn't ever going to eat the prince of pumpkins. Higbee had other plans for it.

It had something to do with my old knotted string.

And sixty-six inches.

CHAPTER 10

"Fire!"

Everyone in town seemed to be yelling that one little red-hot word, running in all directions, and colliding.

Higbee and I had been looking into the store window of Newt's Novelty Shop, at all the grotesque masks. Most of them were priced at a nickel each. Others, a dime. A few of them cost an astronomical fifteen cents . . . a figure way beyond our means.

Hearing people yell "Fire!" we turned around.

As the responsible and helpful citizens of Clod's Corner ran toward the smoke (Higbee and I also ran) I saw several of the Striker gang running away from the fire, and snickering.

"What's burning?" I asked as I ran.

Hig pointed.

"Look. It's that pile of scrap wood at the lumber yard. Wow, what a blaze."

The fire whistle blew.

Seconds later, the wailing scream of a fire engine siren cut through the smoking atmosphere. Around a bend wheezed our one and only red fire truck, ladders rattling, black safety helmets clattering, hoses dragging, and losing three of our firemen at the corner.

I was ready to run to the fire with every other living soul in the town of Clod's Corner but Higbee had other plans.

"Now's our chance," he said.

"For what?"

"To get over to the fire station," said Hig. "There won't be a single solitary person in it."

Over we ran.

Higbee had been correct. Nobody home. The little red station house was deserted. In we sneaked as easily as if we'd been invited. Right through the red door.

"There," said Higbee.

And there it was.

The new bright-red bullhorn was resting on a red table next to Captain José Hosea's red desk. On the desk were pictures of José's wife and his three children, and his faithful dog. A red setter.

Higbee picked up the bullhorn. "I wonder," he

said, "just exactly how this new contraption works."

Raising the mouthpiece to his face, he spoke into the bullhorn. Nothing happened.

"There's a trigger," I said. "See?"

"Ah," said Hig, "so there is." Pulling the trigger, Higbee spoke into the horn, and I thought the walls were going to cave in. "TESTING . . . ONE, TWO, THREE." The noise was almost deafening. "It works," Hig then whispered.

"We better not steal it, Higbee."

"We're not. All we'll do is *borrow* it. In a way, fire equipment is sort of public property. Captain Hosea doesn't own the town fire engine. And the taxpayers, like your folks and mine, helped to purchase this bullhorn. So, as you can see, old top, we are more or less within our rights."

I sighed.

Early in life I had learned that it was futile to argue with Higbee H. Higginbottom. No denying that Hig had a way-above-average brain. In school, Higbee always got A's in every single subject, on every report card. Except once. Only one time did his report card display a B.

Hig had laughed it off.

"We all make mistakes, Quincy, my lad. And this B merely proves that Miss Wiggleton isn't perfect."

CHAPTER 11

Miss Wiggleton smiled.

She was holding a small pumpkin.

"Today," she told us, "is the last day of October. And tonight, will be . . ."

"Halloween," we chorused.

"Indeed," said our teacher. "As you all know, Halloween is a night when strange creatures prowl . . . ghosts, ghouls, and goblins . . . trolls . . . witches and weird wonders."

From the corner of my eye I was watching the weirdest of all . . . Canker, Fester, Hernia, Jaundice, Scurvy, Typhus, and Zitt . . . the sinister seven . . . strange creatures who had been lurking in town for a week.

Higbee winked at me.

"Quincy," he whispered, "today at noon we'll slip our poem into the middle of the Strikers."

I remembered the verse Higbee had written:

Unless you promise never to be mean, your Torture Chamber falls . . . on Halloween.

The Spook

A thought hit me.

It was a very uncomfortable thought, one that slowed my blood, and cooled it. Fact is, at the moment I felt as though I had no blood at all. Instead, I had globs of frozen Prestone.

What, I was wondering, would happen to good old Quincy Cobb (me) if the seven Strikers discovered that I was . . . The Spook?

I knew what would happen, for certain.

The . . . Torture . . . Chamber.

"Higbee," I whispered, "I'm not so doggone sure that I want to be The Spook on Halloween."

"Why not?"

"Well, maybe I'll be a pirate after all."

"Quincy," said Higbee, leaning closer to my ear, "today is no time to decide on, to be or not to be, a pirate. Besides, I have our entire plan already worked out."

"How?"

From his pocket, Higbee produced an object. No, not an object in its entirety. Only half an object.

"Look."

"What is it?" I asked.

"This," he explained, "is a half of a shotgun shell. Late last night, I sneaked downstairs and helped myself to one of Pa's. I cut away half of it. This is what a shotgun shell looks like, inside. It's a cross-section."

"So what?"

"Quincy, see for yourself. This shotgun shell looks very much like the barrel of a cannon. There's a cap, a primer, the main charge of gunpowder, some wadding, and then the slug or the pellets."

"Interesting."

Hig's finger tapped the shell. "Don't you get it, you thickhead? We can rig Big Mouth like this . . . only we shall employ *both* pellets and a slug."

"No, I don't get it. Nor do I want to. You and your crazy ideas always get more and more complicated, and we wind ourselves up in one horrid heap of trouble."

"After school," he told me, "we'll collect more horse chestnuts. My guess is, we really don't quite have enough to fill the barrel."

"Are you nuts? Higbee, we can't mess around with Big Mouth. That cannon may be a fake for good reason. Because if it was real, it could dog-gone blow up the *world*."

Noon time arrived.

Hig pinned his poem to the garbage dumpster, near which the seven Strikers always met. They

74

gathered there in order to determine whose lunch they would steal.

I saw Canker (the only Striker who could read) reciting Higbee's verse aloud to the other six who were punching, biting, cussing, spitting, and kicking each other.

"The Spook," I overheard Canker say.

Right then, I had a suspicion that every Striker eye (all thirteen) was glancing my way, knowing that I was . . . The Spook.

The afternoon dragged.

But it was finally time to leave for home. I knew a minute earlier, as Miss Wiggleton was anxiously eyeing her bottle of Bayer. It wasn't too easily understood why Miss Wiggleton usually looked so . . . so pounded . . . at day's end. We kids did all the work.

"Good-night, Miss Wiggleton," said Hig, as he stood in line at the one door of our little schoolhouse.

"Good-night, Higbee."

I said good-night to her too. And then, Hig and I streaked down the dirt road as if pursued by demons. Or worse, chased by the Strikers. Believe it or not, even Bruto Bigfister sprinted for home.

We stopped for a breather, behind Gridley's Machine Works.

"Quincy," said Hig, "tonight you climb."

"Climb?"

"You climb the pole on the hill. And fly!"

Anyone could have felt it coming. The hot insistent breath of *trouble* was now puffing and panting on the back of my neck.

"Everything'll work out fine," Higbee explained.

"Hold it," I told him.

"What's wrong?" Hig innocently asked.

"It's your *plan*! That's what's wrong. Halloween is tonight. Every kid in town will be at our village square. But not *us*. Where will Hig and Quincy be? I shudder to think. You don't even know yourself. All I wanted to do was go to a Halloween party, have fun, and eat pumpkin pie."

"Pie." Higbee sighed. "It's all too perfect a fit."

We walked another twenty feet, ducked under a fence, and then sat on a couple of big barrels behind Glotzenheimer's Grocery.

"Fit," I said. "I'm about to have one. All I wanted to be was a pirate. But you've talked me into being The Spook."

Higbee nodded.

"Quincy, you'll be not a spook but a star. You and your pillows, flying out of the night."

"Flying?"

Higbee smiled.

"I don't like it," I said. "Down my spine, and up my backbone, I have the chilling sensation that I'm going to get myself hurt."

Hig shook his head.

"No way," he told me. "That's the main reason

we sneaked over to the Frobisher place that night, and bagged all those duck feathers. As you leave the upper telephone pole, you'll have all three pillows around you. For padding. And for dramatic effect, the arms and legs and head of that old drygoods store mannequin. Quince, it's all so very simple."

I poked a finger squarely into Higbee's chest. Not gently. Hard.

"If it's so cussed simple to fly, *you* do it."

Higbee shrugged.

"I can't."

"Why not?"

"Because," said Hig, "somebody has to work the bullhorn. Just before you fly down from the steep hill. On the wire."

I swallowed.

"Come on," he told me. "We'd better head for home, and get our chores done early. Don't bother to eat supper. It'll spoil all that pumpkin pie. Then we'll meet in Mr. Haddock's gully."

"I remember."

"It won't be easy," Higbee said. "But, if all goes according to my mathematical calculations, *pie* will serve our pumpkin."

My brain was spinning.

Higbee was going too fast. Nothing made any sense as far as I could fathom. More than anything, I wanted to be a pirate, Captain Kidd, and then eat a pumpkin pie that Mona May Winker had baked. Yes, and listen to the romantic ballads from Spli-

tlip Schwarzenegger's sousaphone. No, I didn't want the world. Only my own little crumb of Halloween fun.

However, here I was, trudging up Homer's Hill with Higbee H. Higginbottom, heading for home, chores, and supper. And possible disaster.

I wasn't going to be Captain Kidd. Instead, I had to fight a war. As a flyer.

Not as a pirate. I'd be some other weirdo.

A spook.

CHAPTER 12

We met in the gully.

Earlier, I had informed my folks at home that I needed no supper, even though I felt hungry enough to eat my own shoe.

Then I pleaded to be allowed to go into town to attend the Halloween party that Miss Booky had planned. Just for insurance, I mentioned that Miss Wiggleton had urged all of us to attend. Her name would add a pinch of dignity to our overall plan to defeat the Strikers.

Higbee was already there.

"Good," he told me. "You escaped."

Now, I was thinking, if only I could escape the inevitable trouble in which Higbee H. Higginbottom would plunge us.

"Help me," said Higbee.

Squatting, he placed both hands beneath the giant pumpkin, the only pumpkin that Mr. Haddock didn't find and harvest.

"What are we going to do, Hig? Are we going to somehow make this monster into a pie?"

"No. All we have to do is transport this big baby down to the village square, in town."

"Are you nuts?"

Higbee stood up. "Right. I'm nuts. And you're as nutty as I am. Every kid in Clod's Corner is nuts to take punishment from that rotten rat pack of Strikers. Tonight, *we get even.*"

"Okay," I said, recalling The Torture Chamber.

"You're with me?"

I grinned. "To the end." Luckily for me, Quincy Cobb, I didn't know what the ending would turn out to be.

"Heave," said Higbee.

We heaved. The pumpkin wouldn't budge.

Picking up a fallen tree limb, one about as long as a broom, Hig wedged it under the pumpkin. It moved. So I found myself another stick, to pry, and together we rolled it up and out of the little gully. Then under a fence (by digging a depression) all the way down Homer's Hill to the deserted village square. We'd beaten the crowd.

How we did it I will never know.

We even accomplished our miracle carrying rags, a sack of horse chestnuts, three duck-feath-

ered burlap bag pillows, a borrowed bullhorn, and five parts of a discarded mannequin . . . arms, legs, and head.

On no supper.

My empty stomach groaned and growled, telling me it wanted chow. There wasn't any. Except, of course, a raw pumpkin. A huge orange sphere of sustenance. To worsen matters, my nose could smell pies. Scores of them.

Pumpkin pie.

The wondrous smell reminded me of what Mona May Winker had told me. A very extra-special pie was baking, or already baked, and would be coming to the Halloween party. The pleasant fragrance of freshly-baked pie seemed to be wafting from almost every kitchen in Clod's Corner.

"Push," said Hig. "And hurry. People will start appearing here almost any second."

As we were rolling our prize prince of pumpkins along on the grass of the village green, we were about to pass Big Mouth, the great bronze cannon. Higbee stopped. He glanced at the gun's yawning maw, the black hole he'd earlier measured (straight across at its widest) with my length of dirty string.

"Twenty-one inches," Higbee said.

"So what?"

Hig nodded at the pumpkin. "Its exact circumference," he said, "is sixty-six inches. Don't you recall how Miss Wiggleton made pie so simple? It was *twenty-two* over *seven*."

"Is that *pie?*"

"Right," said Higbee. "And this pumpkin is three times that. Sixty-six inches around, in circumference. So, as the cannon's diameter is twenty-one, it's a perfect fit." Higbee paused to take a deep breath. "Now lift."

We strained.

But nothing happened.

"Hey!" I heard a voice. "What are youse two guys doing with that there pumpkin?"

Turning around, I saw him. Somebody who was wearing something very strange around his neck. It was a dog collar. I gulped out his name.

"Bruto Bigfister."

Higbee saw him too. And right then, I gave credit to Higbee H. Higginbottom. He could certainly think on his feet. And fast.

"Bruto, old pal," he said. "All those Strikers are liars. Because what they're telling about you isn't true. And we don't like them."

"Oh yeah?" he snarled. "What'd they say?"

"They said," Hig told him with an honest face, "that you couldn't lift a pumpkin and put it into this hole." He pointed at Big Mouth's mouth. "They claimed you were too weak or too dumb to do it."

I couldn't believe what I saw. Until then, I thought Mona May Winker was a champion pumpkin handler. Then I saw Bruto in action. Spitting on his hands, The Brute bent low, grunted, said a dirty

word, and hoisted up the pumpkin into Big Mouth's gaping hole.

"Bruto," I said, "you're a mighty man."

He glowered at me.

"Is that an insult?" he asked.

"Yes," said Higbee. The dirty rat.

"*No,*" I said quickly. "I meant that you're very strong and powerful. And, because of your help, Hig and I are going to play a prank on the Striker gang."

Bruto smiled.

"Good," he said, "because I hate them kids."

As he spoke, Hig was busily dumping our complete supply of horse chestnuts into Big Mouth's muzzle. Then he stuffed in the rags, using a mannequin leg as a ramrod. Looking inside, I could see nothing at all that would betray what we'd done. Higbee's plan, so far, was really working.

Bruto noticed our mannequin parts, the bullhorn, and the three overstuffed burlap bags, the ones Hig and I had stuffed with duck feathers.

"What's all this junk?" he asked.

"Oh," said Hig, "this is part of our costume for tonight's Halloween party." Hig looked at Bruto. "Hey, Brute . . . how come *you're* not in costume?"

Bruto's eyes narrowed. "I am so. I got this'n around my neck." He pointed at the strange dog collar which was festooned with metal studs and spikes.

"But what *are* you?" I asked him.

83

Before answering, Bruto reached out and grabbed my ear, and Hig's ear. It felt like I'd been suddenly caught between the merciless jaws of a pair of pliers. And it hurt worse than all fury. He wouldn't let go.

"Now," growled Bruto, "youse guys'll know what I am for Halloween." He laughed a mean laugh. "I'm a Doberman *pincher.*"

Bruto left, no doubt to find fresh victims.

My ear was still throbbing, and Higbee was holding his, jumping around. Gradually my pain faded away.

"Quincy," said Hig, "people are starting to arrive for the party. So it's time we took you up the hill to your take-off position."

I sighed.

It was useless to argue with Higbee H. Higginbottom, especially when he was engaged in the execution of one of his master plans.

At the top of the hill stood a telephone pole. It was very old, and gray, and it listed slightly to one side. But all the way up, bottom to top, I noticed this particular telephone pole had metal rungs, for climbing. No spurs needed.

Higbee pointed at the top of the pole. "Up there," he said, "is where you'll start."

"Start what?" I asked him, looking upward.

Pulling a small lanyard hook from his pocket, plus some leather thongs, Hig explained. "All you have to do, Quincy, is wear this harness, hook it to

84

that wire that runs from this pole downhill to the one down there."

"Then what?"

"I'll tie the pillows around you so you'll be fat and well-padded, and I'll also tie these arms, legs, and head on . . . so you'll really look like who you are."

"Who am I?"

"The Spook."

It didn't take Higbee very long to assemble me. There I was, inside the three pillows, a false head above me, mannequin legs dragging below, arms hanging limply on both sides. I was wearing Hig's harness and holding the silver snap hook.

I was ready to fly.

"Remember," said Higbee, "don't slide down the wire until you hear the signal."

"Maybe I won't hear inside all these pillows. What if I can't hear the signal at all?"

"You'll hear it. It'll be very very loud."

"What kind of a signal is it?"

"Big Mouth's *bang.*"

CHAPTER 13

Worriedly I waited.

The sun had disappeared. Halloween night fell upon Clod's Corner; and on *me*, like a fully-loaded railroad car.

Beside me was a useless old telephone pole. Far below, down the steep hill was another. The two obsolete poles were connected by a solitary wire, one that Higbee had decided I would hook to, and slide down. It would look like flying. My three pillows, Hig claimed, would serve to cushion my arrival at the lower pole.

Alone, pacing back and forth, I was pondering the whereabouts of my good old pal, Higbee H. Higginbottom.

He was probably at the party, eating.

86

Below, the Halloween party was almost in full swing. At least a hundred celebrants had arrived. More were coming. A dozen ladies were setting up card tables and placing orange-brown dots on them. I knew what the dots were.

Pie.

Pumpkin pies, my nose informed. Nostrils, I was discovering, can become hungry too.

Yet one of the tables wasn't a square card table. In fact, it was large and circular with nothing on it at all. I wondered why.

Right then, my question was partially answered. A wide flatbed truck wheezed into the area. Gears grinding, it turned around, then backed carefully on the grass where the ladies were decorating the large table. People hurried to the truck. Its round cargo was flatter than a giant pizza and covered by an enormous and billowing white sheet. About twenty men unloaded whatever it was, carrying it gently to the huge table.

No one uncovered the cargo. There it sat, beneath its white cloth covering, remaining a shrouded Halloween surprise.

The Striker gang sneaked over to the big table, but were wisely chased away by guarding adults. I saw Canker, Fester, Hernia, Jaundice, Scurvy, and Typhus.

I couldn't see Zitt.

But I spotted Miss Booky, near the cannon. She was instructing poor Mr. Melvin Murphy, who held

an unlit torch. She gestured at Big Mouth. "Now remember, Melvin, don't torch the primer until I give you the signal. I'll wave my hanky and holler NOW." She paused. "Get it?"

"Got it."

"But," warned Miss Booky, "you mustn't touch off the cannon until I saw NOW."

For *her* sake, I hoped Mr. Murphy would follow instructions. He wasn't the stupidest man in town. Yet nobody ever accused Melvin Murphy of being the brightest.

Everyone was having fun. Kids and adults were dressed as firemen, plumbers, baseball players, clowns, cowboys, and cops. All trying to frighten each other. Sadly, I saw a pirate.

I looked for Mona May Winker.

Because of the darkness I couldn't see too well. In spite of being laden with three large pillows, a fake head, two false arms, and false legs, I climbed up the metal rungs of the telephone pole. Higher and higher, I clanked to the very top, stopping beneath two rotten old spars. To be prepared, I snagged my harness hook to the single wire that stretched diagonally down to the distant pole below.

Then I heard a cheer.

"He's here," people were shouting.

He was indeed. Our star performer from Siberia had at last arrived amid some welcoming tosses of orange and black confetti. (Mr. Murphy lit his

torch, enabling me to see more clearly.) In he paraded, the famous fellow himself, Mr. Splitlip Schwarzenegger, carrying a very large and impressive musical instrument. The biggest silvery sousaphone in the world. Yet, as I could easily notice, Mr. Schwarzenegger wasn't large at all.

He was tiny.

But, despite his lack of size, Splitlip carried his gigantic bass horn as easy as though it were a piccolo. One summer, I'd observed a wee little ant heading for its anthill, toting a prize ten times its size. Splitlip looked like a very determined musical ant.

"Never," my father once told me, "never pick a fight with a small skinny musician. You'll get licked."

Marching boldly to the gazebo Splitlip Schwarzenegger climbed the three stairs with his sousaphone, turned, and sat in the special visitor's chair. The silvery sousaphone gleamed in the moonlight, as did its great golden bell, at the center of which was a black hole where the music would come out. The hole was of considerable size. Larger than a basketball.

Miss Booky cleared her throat.

"Folks," she began, "Mr. Schwarzenegger's opening sousaphone solo will be a classical favorite . . . *Kitten on the Keys*. After which, we shall welcome him for coming with a special one-gun salute." She winked at Mr. Murphy, who held his

burning torch at the ready. Then shook her head, as if to warn him . . . *not now*.

"Here," said Miss Booky, "is our very special treat for *you*, Mr. Schwarzenegger, our honored guest."

She pointed at the large circular table. As she did so, several ladies yanked off the enormous white cloth covering. Wow! There it was for every eye in Clod's Corner to see, and to water every mouth. To rumble every stomach.

A gigantic extra-special *pumpkin pie*.

It was a good twelve feet across. That, as Higbee had taught me, was its diameter. All I'd learned about *pie*.

The crowd quieted with anticipation.

Just as I was wondering what Higbee was doing, I suddenly found out. I heard a booming borrowed bullhorn bellow bombastically:

WARNING . . . WARNING.
YOU STRIKERS HAVE DECIDED TO BE MEAN.
AND SOON . . .
YOUR TORTURE CHAMBER FALLS . . .
ON HALLOWEEN.

It was Higbee's voice.
He paused.

THE SPOOK IS COMING. THE SPOOK.

I heard the lingering echo of Higbee's bullhorn noise fade slowly into a hushed silence. I saw the Strikers, six of the seven, huddle together. Yet nobody spoke.

All of Clod's Corner lay still.

Then I heard one young voice. "I gotcha." It came from far beneath me, at the foot of my telephone pole. Looking down, I saw awful news.

Zitt Striker, the meanest of the seven, stood below, holding a very large axe.

Whack.

My pole shuddered.

Whack. Whack. Whack. Whack.

Zitt was chopping at my telephone pole.

Whack. Whack. Whack.

"Help!" I hollered out. Yet no one could hear me, because down in the gazebo, Mr. Splitlip Schwarzenegger had started to thunder out *Kitten on the Keys.* With every blow of Zitt's axe, I felt the telephone pole becoming weaker . . . and weaker. And I couldn't climb down.

There was only one thing to do.

One route of escape. I took it. Even though I hadn't heard my signal, I let go of the spar and began my suicide slide. In panic, I let out the loudest and most terrible scream of my entire life. Plus the fact that my hook screeched along the wire.

EEEEOOOOWWWWW.

Everyone looked up at me. Yet they didn't see Quincy Cobb. What they saw was a large lumpy

91

thing, a strange hairless head, two dangling arms above two loose legs . . . all flying down at them in the flickering torchlight. They saw The Spook . . . flying!

Children hid.

Ladies wept.

Strong men fainted.

Yet on I flew, down the wire, heading for the lower telephone pole and to what I hoped would be a pillowy stop. The faces that stared at me were all twisted and distorted in total alarm. But only Mayor Doolittle spoke:

"It's . . . it's . . . it's . . . The Spook."

He swooned.

All six of the Strikers ran in terror, fleeing furtively toward their favorite and formidable fort, their shabby shack of shambles, The Torture Chamber. Zitt ran for it too.

Faster I slid. My metal hook scraped along the wire, creating a shower of eerie sparks. And it produced a spooky dead-spirit siren scream. A din that grated a spine like a carrot. Every dog in town started to howl as I slid.

Faster . . . faster . . .

Ahead of me, the lower telephone pole seemed to be growing larger . . . closer . . . *larger* . . . *closer* . . . and closing my eyes I prepared to die. Perhaps my three duck feather pillows would soften the blow.

It came.

WWWHHHHAAAAMMBO.

I hit the top of the pole.

Suddenly it was snowing . . . on Halloween . . . and big feathery flakes of what I thought was a blizzard filled the October evening sky. Up into the air I flew, along with a million duck feathers, my body flipping over and over. I saw sky, then earth. Sky. Earth. Skyearthskyearthskyearth, as I tumbled through space, becoming dizzy. I was flying!

Then I dropped, falling, falling. Somewhere, a long ways off, somebody was playing *Kitten on the Keys*.

And I saw *the moon*.

It was a full moon. Large. Not silvery. This particular moon seemed to be an odd shade of orange-brown and was becoming bigger and bigger . . . and bigger.

KA-PPPLLLOOOOSH.

Pie seemed to be everywhere.

Lots of it somehow splattered into my mouth, and I was chewing, and swallowing. This isn't easily done when you're only half conscious. Feathers fell. All over the place. A stormy sky full of falling duck feathers. But, in my dazed condition, the feathers didn't seem to be that important. So I sat up, in the very center of the largest pumpkin pie ever baked in Clod's Corner, ate, and tried to smile.

The faces that surrounded me were *not* smiling. Many were spitting out duck feathers. One of the faces seemed to be wearing a pumpkin-stained

scowl. I knew whose face it was. Miss Booky's. She was wiping away her anger with a clean white hanky.

"Who . . . are . . . you?" demanded Miss Booky.

I swallowed pie, and answered. "Higbee Higginbottom," I wanted to reply. Yet I didn't. Instead, I gave another name.

"I'm Zitt Striker."

Luckily for me, I was so covered with pumpkin that my own mother and father wouldn't have guessed my identity.

"You," said Miss Booky through gritted teeth, "are about to receive the hottest spanking that your pumpkin-covered behind will ever experience."

I winced. The trouble I was in was far deeper than the giant pumpkin pie.

"And," said Miss Booky, shaking bits of pumpkin pie from her hanky, "you are going to *get it* . . . right NOW."

CHAPTER

14

"Now," said Mr. Melvin Murphy.

I'd just fingered a glop of pumpkin out of my right ear when I heard Mr. Murphy say it. But that was the last word that an entire town would hear.

Big Mouth exploded.

KA-BBBBRRRRROOOOOMMM.

It was obvious, from the sound of the report and the great gray cloud, that nobody had forgotten to load the cannon with gunpowder. Lem Crocker had poured in some. So had Melvin Murphy as well as Osgood Keeler. One charge of black powder would have been adequate. But *three?*

Mr. Murphy, his flaming torch still in hand, was backfired into the air. Prior to this evening, I'd never known that Melvin Murphy could fly. With-

out a wire. Soaring like a kicked end-over-end foot-ball during an extra point, Mr. Murphy disap-peared between two upright elms, perhaps into the upper-row seats of some unseen end zone bleach-ers.

From the front end of Big Mouth it was worse.

Much worse. In a matter of seconds I finally un-derstood what Higbee meant about the *chain*. It was a chain of events, all of them too weird to wit-ness.

First off, a buckeye buckshot barrage pelted the crowd as dozens and dozens of our horse chestnuts whizzed bulletlike. Most of them struck the Stri-kers, who were peeking out from what they imag-ined would be a safe shelter. The Torture Chamber.

Next came the main missile.

A prince of pumpkins.

Amid the smoking rags, out it came, traveling at supersonic speed. Higbee's aim had been accu-rate. The zooming pumpkin smashed into The Tor-ture Chamber.

I'd been to a bowling alley. And watched a ball roll down an alley and crash into ten bowling pins, knocking them every which way. But a bowler's strike was rather tame compared to how a pump-kin cannonball pounded the Striker structure. The boards, crates, garbage cans, a sewer pipe, trash, gasoline drums, and truck tires scattered faster than a flock of flushed vultures.

As many of my duck feathers still fell, Striker

debris rose into a billowing mushroom cloud of dispersing junk.

Ten bowling pins didn't scatter.

But seven Strikers did.

Canker, Fester, Hernia, Jaundice, Scurvy, Typhus, and Zitt were all hollering in horror. Their faces seemed to be expressing that The Spook, whoever or whatever it was, had made good its promise to destroy their filthy rat's nest. And with it, all seven of the rotten little rats.

I had to give our pumpkin credit.

It tore through The Torture Chamber easier than a hot bullet through warm butter. And one thing more. The orange cannonball never stopped. Slowed, oh yes. Stopped? No. Yet it did change course, passing overhead, hissing like a crazed co bra. As it went curving toward one of our town's most revered landmarks, the gazebo, I held my breath. But, up on the gazebo bandstand, Mr. Splitlip Schwarzenegger wasn't holding his.

He was blowing.

Determinedly, the intricate notes and phrases of *Kitten on the Keys* still poured from his massive instrument. Even though, following such a cannonade explosion, few in the park could hear.

Seeing the pumpkin fly toward Splitlip, I wanted to close my eyes.

"Oh, *no*," I thought I heard Higbee say.

SSSSSSSSSSSSCCCHHHWUMMPPP.

Right then, I couldn't believe what I saw. Blink-

ing, I tried to clear my pumpkin-smeared vision enough to witness the greatest baseball play I'd ever seen. What a catch! Without skipping a note, Splitlip leaped up from his chair and caught the orange cannonball. The pumpkin hit the sousaphone's bell hole. Dead center.

Kitten on the Keys abruptly concluded.

Corked.

Miss Booky, several days ago, had informed Higbee and me that Mr. Splitlip Schwarzenegger and his sousaphone never separated. They were always united. Well, perhaps . . . until right now. The great bass horn, with a pumpkin lodged in its bell, was knocked high into the air. Over and over it tumbled, gaining altitude. Then it fell, brushed a maple tree, glanced off the roof of the Methodist church, bounced from the cab of a dumptruck . . . and then crashed in one magnificent landing, into a group of several people. But that was far from all. Expelling out of the sousaphone's bell, with considerable force due to Splitlip's gas buildup inside, the pumpkin popped out like a champagne cork. Then, quite luckily for everybody, the pumpkin stopped when it smacked into one person.

It hit Bruto Bigfister.

I cheered.

With a mouthful of pumpkin pie, cheering is not easily or graciously performed. Yet I cheered with gusto amid a storm of duck feathers that were still softly floating back to earth.

The Striker kids weren't cheering.

They were, as might well be expected, fighting. The fight's purpose was, it seemed, to decide which Striker kid would try to play the sousaphone.

Higbee was cheering too.

But not everybody cheered. Our honored guest, Mr. Splitlip Schwarzenegger, had been knocked off the gazebo. And worse, separated from a most prized possession, his sousaphone, which had fallen into the hands of seven unpleasant children. This was a situation which could enrage, I imagined, any average sousaphonist.

Mr. Schwarzenegger was not average.

"Oh boy," Higbee said. "Here he comes."

Hig was right.

Storming our way charged the tiny musician, rolling up his sleeves, doubling his fists, with a face redder than any maple leaf in October.

"You hellions," he snarled at the Strikers. "When you lived in Siberia you were a bawdy bunch, and here in Clod's Corner, you're worse." Snatching the first Striker he could reach, Canker, our distinguished visitor applied the flat of his talented hand, at impressive speed, to Canker's undefended behind. About a dozen times. Not gently. It was the opposite of *Kitten on the Keys*.

More like a lion on the rat.

What he'd given to Canker, he impartially administered to Fester, Hernia, Jaundice, Scurvy, Typhus, . . . and then to Zitt, who had hidden inside

the golden bell of the sousaphone, where the pumpkin had been. Had the Strikers been duck pillows, he would have spanked the feathers out of all seven.

The entire citizenry of Clod's Corner applauded.

So did Higbee and I.

"Hey." I turned to Hig. "Where in the heck have you been all this time?"

Higbee grinned. "At first," he told me, "when I used the bullhorn, I was hiding, well out of sight."

"Where?"

"In a place I figured would be the last place anybody would think to look . . . in The Torture Chamber."

"Honest?"

"Yup."

"Where's the bullhorn?"

"Quincy, I sort of figured that we'd be safer if I returned it to the fire station. So I did."

I sighed. "Good."

"Say," said Hig, giving me a friendly pat on my pumpkin-soaked back, "that was a super flying job you did, screaming down that wire as The Spook." He smiled. "You deserved to dive into the biggest dessert, and to eat every bite of it."

"Thanks," I said, "but I'd still rather be a pirate."

"I'll be doggoned," said Higbee. He pointed to the seven Striker kids. They weren't fighting, or kicking, or biting anybody. Instead, they were po-

litely helping Miss Booky slice and serve pumpkin pie to everyone.

Zitt was even smiling.

So was I, when I suddenly was aware that the person standing next to me was none other than Mona May Winker.

Higbee eyed Mona May and left.

"Quincy," she whispered, in a voice sweet enough to ooze across a waffle, "I just knew *you* were The Spook." She sighed. "Ohhhh, you're so brave."

"Aw," I said, not knowing quite what to do or say. So I modestly removed a generous hunk of pumpkin pie crust from my hair, and shared it with her.

A crowd of people had gathered around our prince of pumpkins. Higbee was there too. Several folks were commenting that it was, no doubt, the largest pumpkin ever to be grown in Clod's Corner, and perhaps in the entire USA. "Golly," someone said, leaning forward to touch our (or rather Mr. Haddock's) now infamous vegetable, "that thing ought to possibly measure sixty-five inches around."

"Sixty-six," I was compelled to say. "With a diameter of exactly twenty-one inches, a computation that Sir John Napier and I derived by using twenty-two over seven, which, as you all know, is a numerical simplification of . . ."

"Pie," said Higbee. "Happy Halloween."